THE BOXCAR CHILDREN®

CREATED BY
GERTRUDE CHANDLER WARNER

BOOK

160

THE MYSTERY IN THE MAGIC SHOP

ILLUSTRATED BY
ANTHONY VanARSDALE

ALBERT WHITMAN & COMPANY
CHICAGO, ILLINOIS

Contents

1. A Peculiar Mirror   1

2. An Unpleasant Interruption   11

3. The Magician's Code   22

4. Missing Magician   34

5. Retracing Steps   44

6. A Shattering Crash   55

7. The Disappearing Trail   66

8. A Confession   74

9. Henry's Theory   84

10. A New Surprise   93

CHAPTER 1

A Peculiar Mirror

"It certainly is a fine morning," said Mrs. McGregor, the Aldens' housekeeper. She opened the kitchen window to set a cooling pie on the windowsill. The room was bright with sunshine. A small radio on the counter played music.

"Yes, indeed," said Grandfather. He drank the last of his coffee and set his mug in the sink. His four grandchildren finished their orange juice and began clearing the breakfast table. There was a pleasant clattering of cereal bowls, spoons, and plates.

"I have business in Northport for the next few days," he said. Though it was summer Grandfather wore a button-down shirt and a tie. His suit jacket matched his navy-blue slacks.

"You look handsome, Grandfather," Jessie said.

He smiled. "Thank you, Jessie. Do you children need a ride anywhere before I head out?" he asked.

"No thank you, Grandfather," said fourteen-year-old Henry. "We're walking to town for my magic lesson."

"Oh, that's right," said Grandfather. "You've been hard at work all summer, and the show is this weekend. I can't wait to see the tricks you've learned."

"Me either!" said Benny. He was six. He peeked under the table where their wirehaired terrier waited with a wagging tail. Benny snuck him a crust of toast. "Good boy, Watch," he said. "Want to go for a walk?"

Watch jumped and wiggled in a happy circle as Violet went to the back door for his leash. Violet was ten and had used purple ribbons to tie her pigtails today. "Here you go, Watch," she said, clipping the leash to his collar. "Ready?" she called to the others.

Her older sister, Jessie, was wiping the table with a cloth. "Almost done," she said. "Mrs. McGregor, do you need anything from the market? We'll be going that way." Jessie was twelve and liked to help with the cooking and meal planning.

"No, dear, but thank you," said Mrs. McGregor.

***

The Alden children were orphans. When their parents died they learned they had to live with their grandfather they had never met, James Alden. The children heard he was mean, so they ran away to the woods, where they hid in an old boxcar. They made friends with a stray dog and named him Watch. Soon their grandfather found them, and it turned out he wasn't mean at all. He was kind and loving, and he loved their dog too. He brought them to his home in Greenfield, Connecticut, to live as a family. As a special surprise Grandfather arranged for the boxcar to be brought to his backyard so the children could use it for a clubhouse.

Grandfather's home was a few blocks from town. Shade trees lined the sidewalks. Watch trotted ahead of the children as they walked to the Greenfield Magic Shop. A barrel of bright flowers was out front. Next to it stood a life-size cardboard figure of a famous magician, the Amazing Arthur.

He was well-known throughout the state.

Violet said, "Wow, Henry. You're lucky to take lessons from the Amazing Arthur. That's a funny name though. Do you know his real one?"

"I asked him once," replied Henry. "But he wouldn't tell me. He said he likes to be mysterious."

While the children lingered under a tree, Benny pointed to a sign in the window. He was learning to read and liked to practice every chance he got. "'No Dogs Allowed,'" he read, though he had memorized these words weeks ago. He tied Watch's leash to a tree.

"Good boy," said Benny. "We'll be back soon, just like last time." Watch gave one wag of his tail then curled up in the shade. He rested his head on his paw. As his name suggested, he watched the children go inside.

A little bell jingled over the door. Jessie took a deep breath. "I love coming here," she said. "There's always something new."

"Let's look around," said Henry. "My lesson doesn't start for ten minutes."

A few customers were in the store. The Alden

4

children wandered the aisles of colorful displays. There were wooden puzzles, magic wands, decks of trick cards, and rubber snakes and mice. There were magnetic rings to wear on your fingers to hide a metal object in your palm. Draped against a wall were costumes for magicians, with capes and wigs. Rainbow scarves hung from a rafter.

"Hey, wouldn't these be fun?" asked Violet. She shook a tray of plastic ice cubes with pretend spiders inside. "Grandfather would be so surprised when he went looking for ice to make lemonade!"

Jessie momentarily felt alarmed when she noticed a spilled glass of grape juice. But when she touched the liquid, she realized it was plastic. She laughed, thinking it would be a good trick to play on someone with a clean white carpet. She ran her fingers through a box of coins and realized they were also plastic. A wad of fifty-dollar bills turned out to be blank on one side.

"I wonder what Mrs. McGregor would do if she found this pretend money around the house," she said.

"She'd just laugh," Benny said with confidence.

"You're right," said Henry. "Mrs. McGregor loves a good joke. Hey, how about this?" He picked up a rubber tarantula and set it on Violet's head. She plucked it off and passed it to Benny. Benny wiggled its rubbery legs in front of Jessie's face. Jessie snatched it and plopped it on his shoulder.

Benny returned the tarantula to the shelf. He said, "I can't wait to see what tricks you'll perform, Henry. Will you use rubber spiders or rats or a snake?"

"I'm not telling. I'm keeping it a mystery," Henry answered.

The children laughed.

"You're just like the Amazing Arthur," said Violet. "I bet you'll surprise a lot of people."

"Why do you want to learn magic tricks, Henry?" Jessie gave him a quizzical look. "You haven't told us."

Henry smiled. "Okay, I can answer that. You know how Mrs. McGregor always tries to cheer us up when we're grumpy or sad?"

"She makes us popcorn!" said Violet. "She tells funny stories from when she was a little girl. She always makes me feel better. Mrs. McGregor says laughter is the best medicine."

"That's what I think too," said Henry. "Maybe I can visit kids in the hospital and perform some tricks. If I can make them laugh, maybe they'll feel better."

Benny, Jessie, and Violet smiled at their older brother. He was tall for his age and had brown hair like theirs.

"Henry, that is very kind of you—" Jessie began, but a voice from behind the counter interrupted her.

"Ahem!" said an older woman with curly gray hair. She stood with her arms crossed and glared at the four children. Her T-shirt said, "Greenfield Magic Shop, Making Magic Since 1915."

"May I help you with something?" the woman asked. "I'm Mrs. Oliver, the new owner. I haven't seen you kids before. I hope you know this isn't a place to just hang around and touch everything you see."

"Oh, hello," said Henry. He introduced himself and his siblings. "We're waiting for my lesson with the Amazing Arthur. I've been coming here all summer."

"And he's going to be performing in the magic

show this weekend," Benny said.

"That's nice, dear. I haven't seen the Amazing Arthur today," Mrs. Oliver said. "Ever since I've been here, he has always come in late. Honestly I don't know how he expects to keep students. Or this job." She sighed with irritation and turned to help a customer.

While the children waited for the Amazing Arthur, they continued to look at the rows of tricks and gags. Jessie noticed a large mirror at the front of the shop. It was as tall as Henry and as wide as her arm. When she glanced at her reflection, she saw a peculiar ripple in the glass.

"What a strange mirror," she said. "I wonder if it's for a trick." She wandered down an aisle of juggling balls, but she looked back, still curious about the mirror. Suddenly the Amazing Arthur appeared in the mirror! Jessie turned around to see him wave his wand, which was a thin black stick. A plume of smoke rose from its white tip. When the smoke cleared, the Amazing Arthur stood in front of her.

"Hello there, children!" he said. "And a very good morning to you."

The Alden children stepped cautiously toward him. They stared with wide eyes.

The Amazing Arthur smiled at them. He straightened his shoulders, standing as tall as he could. His black satin cape shimmered with tiny stars, and when he waved his arms, the stars sparkled with light. His top hat blinked with colored polka dots.

"Oh!" cried Jessie. "You weren't there a minute ago."

Delighted with his surprise entrance, the Amazing Arthur took a small bow. With his wand he tapped each child on the shoulder and said, "I'm glad to see you!"

CHAPTER 2

An Unpleasant Interruption

Benny knew it wasn't polite to stare, but he couldn't help it. The magician had appeared out of nowhere. Finally he whispered, "How did you do that? That was amazing."

The man grinned. "That's why I'm called the Amazing Arthur."

"But how?" Benny repeated. "One minute you weren't there, and then the next minute you were."

The Amazing Arthur gave the younger boy a wink. "If I told my secrets," he said, "I wouldn't be mysterious, would I?"

Henry turned to his siblings. "I told you he's mysterious."

Mrs. Oliver called out, "Oh, there you are,

Amazing Arthur! I'm trying to keep a schedule here. When you're done with your lesson, I'll need you to run the register. Please remember this is a business, not a magic show."

In a soft voice the magician said, "I'm sorry I'm late again. I'll try to do better."

On the wall behind Mrs. Oliver, framed photos hung next to newspaper clippings about the Greenfield Magic Shop. The oldest article announced the store's grand opening in 1915.

"Is that a picture of your grandfather?" Jessie asked Mrs. Oliver. Jessie indicated a faded black-and-white photo of a magician. He was holding a rabbit in the air with one hand and a magic wand in the other. An upturned hat sat on a table. "Did he really pull a rabbit out of his hat?"

"I can't reveal his trick, but yes, that is my grandfather," Mrs. Oliver replied. "It was a long time ago. When he got old and was too weak to stand up on the stage, he retired. He taught his tricks to my parents and uncles, and they taught me. My mother was my father's assistant."

The Alden children fell silent as they looked

at the many photos. "The whole history of your family is here," said Henry.

"Indeed it is," said Mrs. Oliver. "Magic has been in my family for generations."

Violet pointed to a photo of a young girl with pigtails like hers. The child was petting a white kitten. She wore a black top hat that was a little too big for her and sat lopsided on her head. She appeared to be about six years old, Benny's age. "Mrs. Oliver, is that you when you were little?"

Mrs. Oliver nodded. She seemed to smile at the memory. "With my favorite kitty. As I said it was a long time ago though. Now if you'll excuse me, I have work to do." Mrs. Oliver began cleaning a shelf with a feather duster.

Jessie noticed a stack of flyers on the counter. An announcement printed on blue paper described the upcoming magic show. She picked one up, read it to herself, and then said, "Henry, this says the magic show this weekend will be at the community center. I thought you said you would be performing here in the shop." She held out the flyer to him.

"I did say that," Henry said. He took the flyer

and read it. Then he looked over at the Amazing Arthur. "Isn't that right? The magic show will be here? The flyer also says you'll be performing a new and exciting trick." Then he read aloud, "'Come one, come all. The Amazing Arthur will surprise you by appearing out of thin air!'"

"That sounds amazing," said Violet.

"Out of thin air!" Benny exclaimed. "I can't wait to see that."

"Yes, it'll be great," the magician replied. "I'm certainly eager to show everyone." But when he read the flyer Jessie held, he gasped. "Oh no! There's been a mistake. A terrible mistake."

"No mistake," said Mrs. Oliver.

The Amazing Arthur took a deep breath. He swept his cape over his left shoulder and stood tall. "I don't understand," he said. "Why not have the magic show here, Mrs. Oliver? Why?"

"It's the way I want to do things," she replied.

"But the show has been performed here for years," he insisted. He gestured to the small stage at the back of the shop. A bright red curtain usually hid this stage, but today it was open. A sparkly rope

held it to the side.

"I admit the magic shop isn't large," he continued. "But the town is used to coming here. It's cozy and friendly. There's plenty of room to set up chairs for the audience. All we have to do is move some displays." The Amazing Arthur tried to keep his voice down, but his face turned red with distress.

The Alden children listened. They did not want to interrupt.

"I have my reasons," the store owner said. "Besides, change is good. I'm going to have that little, old stage removed."

The Amazing Arthur removed his top hat. He held it over his heart. "Won't you please reconsider? Your shop is enchanting," he said. "It really sets the mood for kids who come to the show. They like to buy magnetic rings and trick toys with their allowances. As you know it's good for business."

"Nope," she said. She crossed her arms and lifted her chin. "Anyone who wants to buy magic tricks can come here after the show. It's just a few blocks from the community center. That way it won't be too crowded in here."

An Unpleasant Interruption

The Amazing Arthur frowned. His shoulders sagged. A look of hurt passed over the magician's face. "Dear me," he said. "I'm at a loss for words." He pulled a large pocket watch from his vest.

"Wait here, please," he told Henry. "I need to prepare a few things on the stage for your lesson. I'll be right back." The Amazing Arthur's steps were slower than moments earlier when he had appeared out of thin air.

The phone began to ring. Mrs. Oliver set her feather duster on the counter and answered the phone. The children stepped aside to talk among themselves. They didn't want to disturb her.

"Why doesn't Mrs. Oliver want the magic show here?" asked Benny.

"I don't know," said Henry. "She seems frustrated with the Amazing Arthur. And she definitely doesn't want all those people to be here."

"Maybe she's just in a bad mood," said Jessie.

"Or," said Benny, holding his finger in the air as if he'd thought of a good idea, "what if she needs a snack? I get grouchy when I'm hungry. And I sure am hungry now."

His siblings laughed.

"You're always hungry," Violet said.

"You're right about that!" said Benny.

"It's almost lunchtime, Benny," Jessie reminded him. She patted her little brother on the shoulder. "We'll go home while Henry has his lesson. Mrs. McGregor said that pie on the windowsill is for after dinner, but there's plenty of stuff in the fridge to make sandwiches."

The Amazing Arthur came up to Henry. He said, "All right, young man. I'm ready for your lesson. Are you?"

"Yes sir, I am," Henry replied. He waved to his siblings as they left the shop.

The Amazing Arthur led Henry to the stage. Tiny colored lights sparkled against the walls. A small table held a box of props. The Amazing Arthur had left the large red curtain open.

"We'll practice here, Henry," he said. "It's a good way for you to prepare for an audience. When kids and customers start coming in, try to concentrate. Don't let them distract you."

"All right," said Henry. "I just hope Mrs. Oliver

keeps the show here. I like this small stage."

"So do I," said the Amazing Arthur. "Now let's begin."

Henry opened the box of props and pulled out a piece of rope. It was about three feet long. He dangled it in the air. "I almost perfected this last time," he said to his instructor.

"Indeed, you almost did," said the Amazing Arthur. "Do you remember the three most important words for a student?"

"Abra-ca-dabra," Henry answered. Then he laughed. "Abracadabra. Just kidding."

"I know you are, Henry," his teacher laughed. "Your sense of humor will help you be a wonderful magician. As you know laughter—"

"—is the best medicine," said Henry. "And to answer your question, sir, the three most important words for a student are *practice, practice, practice.* Okay, here we go."

Henry demonstrated his trick. He folded the rope in half and held up the closed loop. "I practice at home when my little brother and sisters can't see me. I want them to be surprised this weekend."

"I'm sure they will be." The Amazing Arthur took a pair of scissors out of the box. With a dramatic flair he held them high until the light shined on them. He handed the scissors to Henry.

"Where is he?" A man's loud voice shouted from the store's entrance.

"He can't be bothered," said Mrs. Oliver. "A class is in session."

"I don't care," yelled the man, who stormed up the aisle and onto the stage. The Amazing Arthur and Henry looked up in surprise.

The man wore knee-high boots and a black vest. His white sleeves billowed like balloons. He stomped his foot. "Well, well, well," he said. "It says here you'll be appearing out of thin air." He held up one of the flyers for the magic show. "I want you to tell me everything you're doing."

"Hello Captain Cannon," said the Amazing Arthur. "You shouldn't be here. As you can see I'm in the middle of teaching a lesson. I don't give away my secrets. I won't ask for yours. You know better than to ask for mine. You're a magician yourself, so you should understand the code."

An Unpleasant Interruption

"Is that so?" Captain Cannon stomped his foot again. He jumped off the stage and marched up the aisle. As he left the shop, he yelled over his shoulder, "You'll be sorry! Mark my words—you will regret not telling me."

CHAPTER 3

The Magician's Code

When Henry finished his lesson, he walked home along the shady streets. He found his siblings in the kitchen making sandwiches.

"Lunch is ready!" Benny called. "Are you hungry, Henry?"

"Famished," Henry said. "I really worked up an appetite." He went to the sink and filled four glasses with water. He set them on the kitchen table.

Jessie put sliced apples by each sandwich as the children sat down to eat. "How was your class?" she asked Henry.

"Great, as usual," said Henry. "I'm learning a lot. The Amazing Arthur is so creative, but I still don't know how he'll appear out of thin air."

"Did he give you any clues?" asked Violet.

Henry held up his hand. "First off, you won't believe what happened during class. It was really weird."

Jessie, Violet, and Benny gave their older brother their full attention.

"What happened?" Violet asked.

Henry answered, "Another magician barged right into my lesson. Mrs. Oliver told him to stop, but he didn't. He came up on the stage and made a big scene."

"Yikes," said Jessie.

"It was odd," Henry said. "I was surprised but not in a good way."

"Who was it, and what did he want?" Violet asked.

Henry paused to take a drink of water before answering, "His name is Captain Cannon. He was really mad, and he yelled at the Amazing Arthur."

"Why was he mad?" asked Benny.

"I'm not exactly sure," Henry replied. "But I guess Captain Cannon thinks he should know about the special trick the Amazing Arthur will perform this weekend."

Violet remembered hearing about the magician's code. She said, "Magicians don't like to share their secrets, right? Because then other magicians could use them?"

"Exactly," said Henry. "A special trick wouldn't be special anymore. Anyway, as Captain Cannon was leaving the shop, he said the Amazing Arthur would regret not revealing his secret."

"Uh-oh. That doesn't sound good, Henry," said Jessie. "I hope he doesn't make trouble at the magic show."

"Same here," Henry said. "That worries me a bit."

"Were you scared?" asked Benny.

Henry thought a moment. "Not scared. I just thought it was strange that this grown man was yelling. He looked a bit like a pirate. His outfit, I mean." Henry described the man's tall boots and billowy sleeves.

"A lot of magicians wear a costume," he continued. "It's like they pretend for the stage. The Amazing Arthur told me that's why he likes to flap his cape and do a twirl. It distracts the audience so they won't see what his hands are doing."

Violet said, "Henry, will you show us a trick? Please?"

"Yes!" cried Benny.

"Okay, okay." Henry laughed. He stood up and looked around the kitchen. "I need a helper."

"I'll do it!" Benny raised his hand as if in school.

The siblings pushed their chairs away from the table to give Henry space to move around.

"This is really cool, Henry," said Jessie. "Your first performance, right here in the kitchen. I wish Grandfather were here."

Violet began clapping. "We're ready, Henry. Go for it."

Henry cleared his throat. He put his hands in his pockets. When he removed his hands, he showed them a red metal bottle cap. It was folded in half like a taco. He waved it in the air a few times, then pointed to the sink. There was a dish drainer with cups and bowls drying from breakfast. An empty glass ketchup bottle with its label removed was also drying.

"Benny, see that upside-down bottle?" he asked.

Benny nodded.

"Good," said Henry. "Now please bring it to me."

Benny took solemn steps over to the sink. He carefully took the bottle from the drainer and took it to his brother.

"Now I'm going to demonstrate how to get this—" Henry showed his siblings the red bottle cap in his palm—"into the bottom of this glass bottle." He held up the bottle with his left hand.

"See how the bottom is solid glass?" He tapped it with the metal cap. It made a clinking sound. "The cap can't get inside, right?"

Benny shook his head no. Jessie and Violet also shook their heads. They sat forward in their chairs. They were paying close attention.

"Okay, we're ready," said Jessie.

Henry held the bottle at eye level and shook it with his left hand. "Nothing in it, right?"

"Right," said Violet.

Henry waved the cap in a circle. He tapped the bottom of the bottle with the bottle cap and said, "Ta-da!" Now when he shook the bottle, it rattled. In a dramatic voice he said, "Ladies and gentleman, you can see the cap is now *inside* the bottle!"

Jessie, Violet, and Benny stared in amazement. They didn't know that Henry actually had two bottle caps. The one in his left hand had clung to a magnetic ring on his finger, which he hid in his palm. They also didn't notice that when he tapped the glass bottle with the cap in his right hand, he had slid the cap from his ring into the top of the bottle. While distracting them with the rattling, he had quickly hidden the second bottle cap in his pocket.

"How'd you do that?" Benny asked.

"Wow!" said Jessie.

"Henry, you really can do magic tricks," Violet said. "I'm impressed."

"But how'd you do it?" Benny asked again.

Henry patted his brother on the back. "You're a good sport, Benny, but remember the magician's code. I can't tell you."

"Do another one," said Violet.

Henry looked at the clock above the sink. "There are some things I need to do first," he said. "But... hmm...actually I could use your help preparing for my show, Violet. Your help too, Jessie and Benny.

Would that be okay?"

"Of course," said Violet.

"Count me in." Jessie gave a thumbs-up.

"Me too!" said Benny.

"Okay, good," said Henry. "Meet me in the boxcar in ten minutes."

***

The boxcar sat in Grandfather's backyard among a grove of trees. In winter the trees sheltered the boxcar from blizzards, and in summer they provided shade, as they did today. The boxcar was in the shape of a rectangle, with two short sides and two long sides. Its iron wheels were partly dug into the ground to keep it from rolling away. A little white porch had three steps, and a pot of red flowers sat on each step.

Jessie stepped up to the wide metal door. With an *oomph* she slid it open. A worktable in the center of the boxcar held baskets of paint brushes, pens, and other art supplies. A hammer, nails, scissors, and hand tools were tucked into cubbies along one wall.

As planned Henry met his siblings in their

clubhouse ten minutes later. They greeted him with smiles.

"Reporting for duty," Benny said. He gave a little salute.

"I like how you are always ready to help," Henry said.

"So how can we help?" Jessie asked.

"Okay, first I need a magic wand," Henry began. "It can be almost anything. A chopstick, a skinny pole, something like that. I'm not exactly sure how I'll use it, but I know it'll come in handy as I learn more tricks."

Benny dashed out into the yard. He called over his shoulder, "Back in a minute!"

"Next I need a magician's box to hold my props," Henry said. "The Amazing Arthur has a really cool one made from wood. It's like a small treasure chest, but I don't need one that fancy."

It was Violet's turn to spring into action. She rummaged through a cupboard until she found a shoebox full of pencils and crayons. She dumped them into a basket. "Will this work, Henry?" she asked, holding up the shoebox.

"Perfect!" he answered.

Now Henry looked at Jessie. "I need a table for practicing my act. I won't need it at the show because the Amazing Arthur has one I can use."

Jessie snapped her fingers. "How about these?" Two plastic tubs stacked against a wall were the height of a small table. The tubs held picnic gear from their last trip to the lake.

"Good thinking!" said Henry. He helped Jessie empty the tubs. They arranged masks and snorkels, beach towels, and campfire equipment onto a shelf.

The Alden children spent the afternoon with their projects.

Benny finished first. "Ta-da!" he exclaimed. He presented his brother with a foot-long twig he had found under a tree. He had painted the tip white. A colorful swirl of ribbons adorned the stick.

"This is the best magic wand I could ever have," Henry said. "Thank you, Benny!"

Violet presented her project next. "Your magician's box," she said proudly. She had drawn stars and little sparkly fairies along each side of the shoebox. Rose petals and daisies from

Grandfather's garden were glued onto the lid. In her beautiful penmanship she had written "Henry the Magician."

"I love it, Violet. It's the perfect size," Henry said. "Not too big. Not too little. Thank you. And now," he said, "here's what Jessie and I have been working on."

The stacked tubs came up to Henry's waist. "Oh, one more thing," Jessie said. She hurried outside and ran to the house. She returned with a checkered tablecloth from the kitchen, which she then draped over the top. It touched the floor so the tubs were hidden from view.

"Ta-da!" said Jessie. "Henry's magician's table. It'll be out here for when you want to practice."

The children admired their work. Afternoon sunlight poured into the old boxcar. The breeze kept them cool.

***

After dinner the children took Watch to the park. The pool was bustling with families enjoying an evening swim. The tennis courts were also busy. While the Aldens played fetch with Watch, they noticed an old truck pull up to the community center. It parked in the loading zone. The driver got out and began carrying boxes into the building. He kept looking over his shoulder as if he were worried about being seen.

"Hmm," said Jessie. "Does that man look nervous to you?"

"He does," Violet said.

"Can we go see what he's doing?" Benny asked Henry.

"It'll be dark soon, Benny," Henry answered. He whistled for Watch, then clipped the leash onto his collar. "We should get home before Mrs. McGregor worries."

CHAPTER 4

Missing Magician

The next morning the Alden children walked downtown to the Greenfield Magic Shop. As they passed one of the cafes, they could smell the pleasant aroma of pancakes and bacon. A nearby newspaper stand offered an early edition. The headline read, "Greenfield's Magic Show this Weekend. An Annual Tradition."

"Hello, Mrs. Oliver," Henry said when they entered the store. "I'm a bit early for my lesson. Do you mind if we just look around?"

"Suit yourself," she said. "But the Amazing Arthur isn't here. Not only that, he missed his eight o'clock class. I honestly don't know what's going on with him. He's in charge of the magic show too.

Last night I had to remind him to drop off supplies at the community center."

"Oh! We may have seen him," Jessie said, "but he wasn't wearing a cape or top hat. Does he drive an old truck?"

"I don't know. Maybe," said Mrs. Oliver. "He was upset about taking things over there. When he came back he asked me again to have the magic show here in the shop. He stood right here by the cash register and practically begged me. I said no. I turned away for just a second, but when I looked back he had vanished."

"Vanished?" asked Henry.

"Gone. Just like that." Mrs. Oliver ran her fingers through her gray curls. She seemed nervous. "Here one moment, gone the next. If I didn't know better, I'd say the Amazing Arthur pulled a disappearing act."

"I'm not surprised," a voice said from one of the aisles. A man in a pirate costume came up to the counter. It was Captain Cannon. He carried a shopping basket with a large rubber sword inside.

"The Amazing Arthur is a huge disappointment,"

said Captain Cannon. "If he doesn't show up soon, I'll take over the magic show. He doesn't deserve to be in charge."

"Why do you say the Amazing Arthur doesn't deserve to run the magic show?" Henry asked.

"Oh, that's easy," Captain Cannon replied. He added a tube that resembled a spyglass to his shopping basket. "He wouldn't tell me about his new trick. I don't think he can pull it off. And I'm the best magician around. The best. Period."

Mrs. Oliver rang up his purchase. "Better or best, I don't care. I never wanted to sponsor the magic show in the first place. The Amazing Arthur was behind the show, and if he doesn't turn up I'll cancel it."

"Is that so?" Captain Cannon stomped his boot. "It cannot be canceled. Everything's planned. It'll be a fabulous show." In a menacing whisper he repeated, "Don't forget, I'm the best magician around! The best."

The Alden children stepped into another aisle where tall shelves gave them privacy to talk.

Violet said, "What did he mean by 'everything's planned'?"

"Maybe he just means that flyers have been printed," Jessie suggested. "And everything's set for the magic show to be held at the community center."

"But what if Captain Cannon had something to do with the Amazing Arthur's disappearance?" Benny asked.

"It definitely seems like there's a rivalry between them," said Henry. He glanced around the shop. "But we don't know for sure that the Amazing Arthur is missing. Maybe this is part of his new trick. What do you think?"

"I don't know," said Violet. "Why would he miss your lesson on purpose? He's never done that before. And why would he miss the other lesson this morning?"

"Good questions," said Jessie, pulling out her notebook to jot them down.

"I just hope nothing has happened to him," Henry said.

Suddenly Benny rushed to the front of the store.

"Hey, Benny, what's up?" Violet called.

"Look!" Benny shouted. "It's gone!"

"What's gone?" Henry asked him.

"The mirror," said Benny. "I just noticed that the big mirror we saw yesterday is gone! It's the one the Amazing Arthur suddenly appeared out of. Remember?"

"Remember? Yes! How could we forget?" said Jessie. "But where did it go?"

Benny turned his palms up in question. He went over to the counter. "Excuse me, Mrs. Oliver.

Did you happen to move the mirror that was here yesterday?"

Mrs. Oliver also seemed baffled. She shook her head. "I think it was here last night when I closed the shop and locked up. I can't believe I didn't notice earlier that it had been moved. Gosh, I've been distracted."

"Maybe it's a clue to where the Amazing Arthur is this morning," said Henry.

"Oh honestly," said Mrs. Oliver. "If there's any more trouble around here, I'll just cancel the show. As I told you kids, I never wanted to sponsor it in the first place."

"I hope you don't cancel it," said Benny. "Magic shows are lots of fun. Kids will want to come into the shop to buy things." He picked up a magician's wallet with secret pouches. "We like stuff like this."

"I agree with Benny," Violet said. She went to the rack of books and magazines about magic. "Magic is fun, Mrs. Oliver. Pretending is fun. Even if kids just buy one magazine, they might come back again and again. Wouldn't the show help business?"

Mrs. Oliver waved her hand as if shooing flies. "It's my decision. Run along now. I have work to do. You can wait on the stage if you want. I trust you not to run around up there and make a mess."

The Alden children went over to the small stage. Folding chairs were stacked against the wall.

"Everything looks the same as yesterday," Henry said.

"What are we looking for?" Benny asked.

"I'm not sure," replied Henry. "Some kind of clue. I just wonder if this is part of the Amazing Arthur's new trick. The big one he won't tell anyone about. As we know, he's famous for being secretive."

"That's for sure," Violet agreed.

"*Or*," said Jessie with emphasis, "what if Captain Cannon has something to do with this? He just told all of us that he wants to take over the magic show. He's super unfriendly."

Henry thought a moment. "It's possible."

"I've been wondering something," said Violet. She pointed to the counter where Mrs. Oliver and Captain Cannon were still talking. "What if Mrs. Oliver is involved? She doesn't want to have the magic show here. I can't figure out why, but she's grumpy about it and is willing to cancel the whole thing."

Benny crossed his arms and nodded. He narrowed his eyes and said, "Yep. Something's definitely going on."

Henry stepped off the stage and went to a side door. He jiggled the latch. The door creaked open. "Hey, look at this," he said.

"Where does it lead?" Jessie asked him.

"To the alley behind the shop," said Henry. He looked left then right, squinting in the bright sunshine. Then he looked at the doorknob. "There's a keyhole on both sides. Since Mrs. Oliver locks up when she closes the shop, it means the Amazing Arthur couldn't have gone out this way last night without a key."

"You're right!" Violet said.

The children continued to look around. They searched in corners full of costumes and hats and among the stacked chairs for anything out of the ordinary. Finally Henry checked his watch. He said, "Well, it looks like the Amazing Arthur isn't coming for my lesson. We should get going."

"Let's ask Mrs. Oliver one last question," said Jessie.

The store owner was at the counter, arranging a rack of glow-in-the-dark wands. "I see you kids are leaving," she said. "If the Amazing Arthur ever shows up, I'll tell him you were here. And that you waited longer than most patient adults would."

"Thank you, Mrs. Oliver," Henry said. "We're curious about a couple more things though. Is it possible the Amazing Arthur let himself out the front door last night when your back was turned?"

"Nope," she replied. "I didn't see him. At night I would have heard that little bell jingling if he opened the door even a few inches. During the day so many people are coming and going that I barely notice it."

Jessie looked toward the front of the shop where they'd last seen the mirror. "Then do you have any idea how the mirror disappeared?" she asked. "Or when?"

"No idea," replied Mrs. Oliver. "When I took over this store, I changed the locks. I didn't give out any new keys, so I can't imagine how anyone got in here last night to take the mirror."

The Alden children exchanged looks of bewilderment.

As they walked out Henry said, "So the mirror has disappeared. And so has the Amazing Arthur."

CHAPTER 5

Retracing Steps

Before dawn the next morning, Henry and Watch went outside to the boxcar. It was dark and Henry's siblings were still sleeping. He wanted to practice his tricks without them seeing how he did them.

He turned on a light, and then he set his magician's box on the worktable. Henry removed the lid Violet had decorated and took out a short strand of rope.

"Okay, here we go," he said to Watch. But the terrier was staring at the door. Watch cocked his head with curiosity. He didn't bark or growl when someone knocked.

Henry slid open the door. In the light shining

from the boxcar, he could see Mrs. McGregor on the little porch.

"Good morning, Henry," she said. She held a tray with hot chocolate and a chunk of warm bread with butter melting in its center.

"Mrs. McGregor, hello! Come in."

"You're up quite early," she said. "I wanted to give you a little something to start your day."

"Wow, this is great," he said. "Thank you"

"You're most welcome, Henry."

"Mrs. McGregor, I'm sorry if I disturbed you when Watch and I dashed through the kitchen."

The older woman smiled. She said, "Not at all, dear. I was busy taking bread from the oven."

"Mmm. It's so good," he said. "I wanted to practice before the others wake up."

"Good for you, Henry."

"It's hard but fun. I think I get a little better every day. You probably already know what the Amazing Arthur says: 'Practice, practice, practice.'"

"I do indeed," she replied. "That's how I've learned to cook. I've been practicing all these years. Well, I'll leave you to it, Henry."

"Thank you again, Mrs. McGregor."

"By the way," she said, stepping down from the boxcar's porch. "While I was mixing up your hot chocolate, I heard some odd news on the radio. The Amazing Arthur is missing."

Henry's face turned serious. "Really? It was on the radio?"

"Yes, in between my favorite music. The report also mentioned the strange timing with the magic show just two days away."

"The Amazing Arthur didn't show up to my lesson yesterday," Henry told her.

"My goodness," she said. "What do you think happened?"

"We don't know, Mrs. McGregor. I'm supposed to have another lesson today."

"Try not to worry, Henry."

"I'll try." He took a sip of hot chocolate. "This is really good. I mean it."

During their conversation Watch had been sitting on a little rug. He kept his eyes on the housekeeper, his right front paw up in the "please?" position. His tail wagged ever so slowly.

Retracing Steps

The housekeeper smiled at the polite terrier. "Oh, all right," she said. She reached into her apron pocket and took out a dog biscuit. Watch gently accepted it then took it to a corner where he could enjoy it at his leisure.

Mrs. McGregor laughed. "Watch knows I always have something for him. See you later, Henry. We're having scrambled eggs and oatmeal this morning in an hour or so."

Henry watched her go into the kitchen. A light by the stove flicked on as Mrs. McGregor began making breakfast.

***

After breakfast the children took Watch for a walk. The morning was already warm, promising a hot summer day. In the park there was a large fountain with water shooting up from the ground. Young boys and girls and a few dogs were running through the spray to cool off.

A woman pushing a baby carriage was talking to her friend. "Missing," the young mother said. "How can a magician go missing?"

Two men in jogging shorts ran by. One said,

"He's been performing for years." The other man said, "A very important part of our community," before they jogged out of earshot.

The Alden children looked at one another with concern.

Benny asked, "Is everyone talking about the Amazing Arthur?"

"It seems like it," said Henry.

They continued into town. They passed the donut shop, the bookstore, and a coffee kiosk.

The barista's little radio was playing music. Soon a newscast interrupted. "With Greenfield's annual magic show just two days away," the radio voice said, "what will we do without our magician?" The newscast continued to describe the mysterious disappearance of the Amazing Arthur.

Henry looked at his brother and sisters. "This is really serious."

"Henry," said Benny, "are you worried?"

"I'm starting to be."

"What if it has something to do with Captain Cannon?" Violet wondered. "He threatened the Amazing Arthur about his new trick. Remember?"

Retracing Steps

"I think Mrs. Oliver is involved," said Benny. "She doesn't like the Amazing Arthur."

Jessie said, "I agree. Something's not right with Mrs. Oliver."

"I have an idea," said Henry. "Let's try to retrace the Amazing Arthur's steps from when I last saw him during my class the other day."

The children kept walking toward the magic shop. Sidewalks were busy with the usual shoppers and neighbors greeting one another. Watch trotted on his leash, perfectly behaved. The terrier seemed to understand he was part of an important mission.

"Okay, Henry," Violet said. "So going back to the other day, you came home from your lesson. We ate sandwiches at the kitchen table."

"Then you showed us that trick with the bottle cap," Benny said. "I liked it."

Henry ruffled his brother's hair and smiled. "Thanks, Benny. All right, let's keep thinking."

Violet counted on her fingers. "After dinner we took Watch to the park. We saw someone unloading boxes at the community center. It looked like a man, and it looked like he was nervous. Remember how he kept looking over his shoulder?"

"That's right," said Jessie. "And Mrs. Oliver told us she made the Amazing Arthur take stuff over there. Was he that person?"

"I think it's possible," Henry said. "And if it *was* the Amazing Arthur, what did he do next?"

"Well, hmm," said Violet. "Remember what Mrs. Oliver told us? She said he came back from the community center to the shop. He was upset. He wanted her to change her mind."

"These might be important clues," Jessie said as she opened her notebook. "Let's try to figure out where he went after he talked to her."

The sidewalk in front of the Greenfield Magic Shop was cool with shade. The cardboard cutout of the Amazing Arthur was still there. Violet helped Watch get settled under a tree. When she noticed the newspaper stand she said, "Benny, can you read that headline? The one in big print?"

Benny took a serious look. Sounding out the letters to himself, he finally said, "Missing! The Amazing Arthur is missing!"

"Perfect, Benny. Good job," said Henry.

When they went inside they saw more customers than usual. Some unruly children were running up and down the aisles shrieking. One tossed juggling balls in the air but dropped them. Another threw a rubber tarantula to a girl who threw it back. "Kids, kids, stop it right now!" yelled a man struggling with a toddler in his arms.

The Aldens found Mrs. Oliver pacing behind the counter. She held a copy of the newspaper. "This is getting out of hand," she said to a customer. "How dare the Amazing Arthur pull this stunt. If he ever shows up, I'm going to give him a piece of my mind."

Mrs. Oliver quickly softened. "I mean as long as he's okay and nothing tragic has happened to him. Are you here for another lesson?" she asked when she saw Henry.

"I hope so," he answered. "But we heard on the radio that the Amazing Arthur has disappeared. People are talking and worrying. It's become a big deal." He stepped closer so he could talk to her without the whole store listening in.

"Mrs. Oliver, you said you don't want the magic

show here at the shop, but could you help us understand why?"

"I'm new at running this business. I want it to be the best magic store in the state of Connecticut. But it is a business and not a theater. And now with the Amazing Arthur's disappearance, I don't have any help around the shop. I've been so busy I forgot an important order, and customers were very upset." Mrs. Oliver's cheeks went red with frustration. "I don't want to run a theater. That's why I want the event at the community center. There's better seating in the auditorium. The stage has an automatic curtain that opens and closes when you push a button. There are public restrooms and water fountains.

"Another thing," Mrs. Oliver said. Her voice shook with anger as she patted the counter. "Remember my flyers? The stack I had here, right by the register?"

"Oh, yes. We remember," said Violet. "They were on blue paper. Did they get passed around already?"

"Hardly," answered Mrs. Oliver. "Someone took

them. The whole bunch."

"Oh no! That's awful," Jessie said.

"Well," said Mrs. Oliver with a sigh. "Perhaps it's for the best. I've wanted to cancel the show anyway." She turned away from the children and hurried into the storeroom.

CHAPTER 6

A Shattering Crash

The Aldens left the noisy magic shop. They stood out front on the shaded sidewalk and drank from a water fountain. The day was getting hot.

"Mrs. Oliver is really upset," said Violet as she untied Watch from the tree.

"She sure is," Jessie agreed. "I don't blame her. The Amazing Arthur disappeared without telling her anything. He's supposed to help her in the shop and give magic lessons."

Benny said, "And someone took all her flyers. Who would do that?"

The children crossed the street in a crosswalk. They were taking Watch to the park again because he'd been sitting so long.

Henry said, "News all over town has brought publicity, but it's distracting. It made her forget an order."

"And did you see all those little kids running around?" Benny asked. "I would never do that."

His older brother and sisters smiled at him.

"We know you wouldn't, Benny," said Jessie.

As they reached the park, Henry unclipped Watch's leash. Watch cooled his paws in the giant splash pad and had a good long slurp of water. He shook his wet fur. The Aldens dashed with him through the jumping plumes of spray to cool off. They ran across a soccer field, passing the tennis courts and playground. By the time they reached the community center, they had dried off.

The building had its own parking lot. But at this hour there were no cars or trucks. "I wonder when it opens," said Henry as they neared the front door. "Benny, can you read the sign?"

Benny stood on his toes to see the small print. "'Twelve o'clock noon,'" he read.

"Good job, Benny," said Jessie. She tugged at the wide glass door. "Locked. Should we come back after lunch?"

A Shattering Crash

But Henry was walking around the side of the building. Near the loading dock he said, "This is where that person was carrying stuff the other night."

A narrow door below an exit sign was propped open. A small chunk of wood held it open wide enough for a person to slip through.

"Looks like someone's here," Violet said in a quiet voice.

"Can we go in?" whispered Benny.

"I don't see a sign that says we can't," said Violet. "So I guess it's okay."

Benny tied Watch to a shady tree. "Stay here, boy. We'll be right back."

The Aldens cautiously stepped inside. Their footsteps echoed in the entryway.

"Hello?" Henry called. "Is anyone here?"

A janitor at the far end of a hallway waved to the children. He was pushing a broom across the tiled floor.

"I'm in the magic show this weekend," Henry told him. "Would it be okay if we looked at the stage?"

"Help yourself," the janitor said.

The community center was dark except for

windows that looked out onto the sunny park. Jessie opened a set of double doors with a loud *clunk*. It was the auditorium. Rows of seats sloped down toward a wide stage. The room resembled a movie theater.

Henry drew in his breath. "So this is where Mrs. Oliver wants the magic show. The stage is huge compared to the one in the magic shop."

"Would you be nervous being up there by yourself, Henry?" Violet asked.

"I think so!" he answered. "What if I make a mistake? Or what if one of my tricks doesn't work? People will laugh at me."

"I don't think they will, Henry," said Jessie. "People are nice when kids try new things. How many tricks are you going to do?"

"Just two," he replied.

"Can we see which ones?" asked Benny.

"Well..." Henry thought a moment. "Let's look around here first."

They peeked backstage. There were several boxes with their tops ripped open.

"Hey, look," Benny said. "These are the boxes we

saw the other night."

"How can you tell?" asked Violet. "It was dark."

Benny pointed to a stamped label on each carton. "'Greenfield Magic Shop,'" he proudly read.

"Oh! You're right, Benny," said Violet.

They looked through the boxes.

"These are props for the magic show," Henry said. "Lots of 'em."

"Can you tell us what tricks they're for?" Benny asked.

Henry held up a cardboard tube that had once held wrapping paper. "This is a Magic Cylinder. It's empty now, but things will appear inside."

"But how does it work?" Benny asked.

Henry just smiled.

Jessie unpacked a box of stars cut out from construction paper. They were assorted colors and had numbers on one side. "How about these?" she asked.

"Mind reading," Henry answered.

"But how do they work?" Benny asked again.

"Magic," said Henry.

Benny pouted.

"Okay, I'll show you one trick." Henry pulled out a cowboy hat. With his other hand at the bottom of the box, he gathered up several scarves. He did this so quickly, his siblings didn't see what he had done. Then he secretly tucked the scarves into his palm.

"Don't look at me until I tell you," Henry instructed. He turned his back on them. Now he squished the scarves into a small pocket hidden inside the hat.

"Okay, now you can look." Henry put on the hat, turned around twice, then whipped it off his head. He rotated it this way and that way. He turned it upside down to show that the cowboy hat was empty. Since the pocket holding the scarves was camouflaged, Jessie, Violet, and Benny could not see where the scarves were hidden.

Now Henry waved his hand over the hat. "Abracadabra!" he cried. He slowly pulled out a red scarf. It was tied to a blue one, which then emerged from the hat. A green one followed, then orange, then a purple one. He kept pulling until all the scarves were out. He waved them in the air like a colorful kite.

"Wow!" Benny cried. "How'd you do that?"

Once again Henry just smiled. "Magic," he said.

"Now I understand," Jessie remarked. "You can tell us what these things are for. And you can perform the trick. You just can't show us how they work."

"You're honoring the magician's code," Benny said.

"That's exactly right," said Henry.

"What are you supposed to do if you goof up on stage?" Benny asked. "In front of all those people staring at you?"

"That thought scares me," Henry admitted. "But you know what the Amazing Arthur told me?"

"What?" his siblings said at once.

"To just keep going. Keep up the patter."

"Patter?" Benny asked.

"That's where you say things like 'Ladies and gentlemen!' or 'How're all you folks doing today on this splendid afternoon?' You keep talking so they don't notice you dropped the deck of cards or forgot to roll the dice."

Jessie said, "Patter away, Henry."

"I need to practice that too," he said.

A Shattering Crash

Violet went to the center of the stage where she could look out over the rows of seats. A huge clock was high up on the far wall. "Hey everyone," she called. "It's eleven thirty. This place opens in half an hour. We're running out of time. If we don't find the Amazing Arthur, Mrs. Oliver will cancel the magic show! She won't even let Captain Cannon take it over."

A sudden crash echoed through the empty auditorium.

Benny jumped. "What was that?"

"It sounded like it came from over there," Jessie said.

The Aldens carefully stepped backstage. A large mirror had fallen to the floor and shattered.

Thousands of sharp pieces of glass were strewn across the floor.

Jessie grabbed the back of Benny's shirt. "Careful!" she said.

"Is that the mirror from the shop?" Violet wondered.

"Uh-oh, I think it is," said Henry. "The one the Amazing Arthur suddenly appeared in front of the other day. I still don't know what trick this mirror is used for. He didn't explain."

Jessie carefully pushed the toe of her tennis shoe through the broken glass. "I bet it's for the new trick he was going to unveil. We didn't see him—or that person—the other night carrying in a big mirror. But if this is it, the Amazing Arthur must've been planning to be at the magic show, even if it's held here at the community center."

Henry said, "The Amazing Arthur wouldn't have left town if he was planning to be at the show, right?"

"Right!" Jessie agreed.

Benny stepped around the shattered mirror and into the hallway by the door where they had entered. He held the door wide open. The bright sunlight revealed something new.

Spots of red paint had dribbled from the mirror out through the door. "Someone spilled paint," Violet said.

Jessie leaned closer. "Uh, that's not paint," she said. "I think it's blood. It's a deep red, kinda oozy-looking."

A Shattering Crash

"Blood?" Benny cried.

Henry bent down for a better look. "I think it's blood too. Whoever was just here must have knocked over the mirror."

"And must have gotten cut on the glass," Jessie said.

"But who?" Violet asked. "I hope it's not a serious cut."

Henry stood up. "Me too. Let's keep looking. We need to find out who was here. But first let's let the janitor know about this dangerous mess before someone else gets hurt."

CHAPTER 7

The Disappearing Trail

Benny was first out the door of the community center. Violet followed, then Jessie and Henry.

"The trail goes this way!" Benny shouted. He hurried to unclip Watch from his leash and then untied the leash from the tree. He patted the terrier on the head and then pointed. "Good boy, Watch. See these bloody drops? Show us where they go."

Watch looked up at Benny in earnest. He wagged his tail then took off in the opposite direction. He had seen a squirrel.

"Wait, come this way!" called Benny.

"He's not a tracking dog," said Jessie. "Let's go. He'll come back in a minute."

The children followed a fading trail of blood.

The Disappearing Trail

It looked like the person had been running. The children kept their heads down and stepped carefully around the spots. They went through the parking lot and then onto the sandy volleyball court where Watch caught up to them.

"Over here!" shouted Violet. "This way, toward the soccer field!"

Just as they ran onto the grass, the park's sprinkler system splashed on. The field suddenly became drenched, as if a summer raincloud had burst.

"Oh no!" Henry yelled above the noise of swishing sprinklers. He looked down. "We've lost the trail. It's being washed away."

"How can we follow something that's not there?" said Violet.

"We can't," Jessie said. "It's like trying to find the Amazing Arthur when we don't know where he went."

For several minutes the Alden children watched the sprinklers. Sunlight sparkled through the plumes of water. Mist cooled them off.

Finally Violet said, "Is anyone else hungry?"

"I am!" yelled Benny. "It's lunchtime, right?"

"Yep," said Henry. "How about that little cafe Grandfather likes to go to when he's in town? It'll only take us a few minutes to walk there."

"I love that place. Let's go!" said Jessie.

***

The Bluebell Cafe was on a quiet side street. A striped awning protected the entrance from the hot sun. A teenage boy in a blue T-shirt greeted the Aldens with menus. He wore a black sash around his waist as an apron. "Patio or inside?" he asked them.

"Patio, please," said Jessie. "For our dog." Sitting outside would also help them all dry off after being splashed by the sprinklers.

"Okay, awesome," the boy said. "Come this way." He led them to a table under a large blue umbrella. "I'll be right back to take your order," he said. Watch settled himself in the shade near a splashy fountain. Below it was a water bowl with a sign.

"'Dogs welcome,'" Benny read. "No wonder Watch likes to come here."

After the children ordered lunch, they discussed the case.

"We already had a lot of questions," Jessie began. "And now we have the broken mirror to wonder about. Do you think it has anything to do with the Amazing Arthur's disappearance?"

Henry said, "Actually I do. For one it was in the magic shop that day he suddenly appeared in front of it, out of nowhere."

"But now it's shattered and completely useless," Violet said. "I wonder who was there. And why did they leave in such a hurry?"

"Could someone else be looking for the Amazing Arthur?" Henry wondered.

"What if it was the Amazing Arthur himself?" Jessie asked.

The teenage boy rolled out a tray to their table. He passed around blue plastic baskets with their wrapped cheeseburgers and pickles. Another basket held hot, crispy French fries. The boy set tall creamy milkshakes by each of the Aldens. "Have a nice lunch," he said. He pulled a bottle of ketchup from his apron and placed it on the table before turning to go. "Just holler if you need anything else."

"Thank you," the children said.

"I think the mirror is connected to the new magic trick," said Violet. "The one the Amazing Arthur was planning. He was very secretive about it. And Captain Cannon threatened him. He really wanted to know how it would work."

Jessie took a small notebook from her pocket. She liked to keep track of clues by writing them down. Clicking her pen, she said, "Okay, we know that the Amazing Arthur likes making an entrance. He's famous for making a big dramatic splash. So just plain disappearing isn't his style."

"Right," said Violet. "He loves an audience to applaud and cheer him on. When he vanished the only person who could have possibly seen it was Mrs. Oliver. Why would he do a trick with only one person to notice?"

"These are good questions," said Jessie. "So what happened to him?"

Henry squeezed ketchup on his fries and put the basket in the center of the table to share.

"I think Captain Cannon is probably involved. He's a big show-off and is bossy. I witnessed how mean he was to the Amazing Arthur," said Henry. "And he accused the Amazing Arthur of not being able to perform his new trick just because the Amazing Arthur wouldn't break the magician's code."

Benny said, "And don't forget he said the Amazing Arthur would regret not telling him the secret. Isn't that what he said, Henry?"

"That's what he said," Henry replied.

Benny ate the whipped cream off his milkshake and the cherry on top. Then he poked a straw into the ice cream. After a big swallow he said, "I also think Mrs. Oliver is involved."

"Really? Why?" asked Violet.

"She's mean," Benny answered.

"Being mean doesn't make her guilty," said Jessie. "Remember how upset she was about all the stuff going wrong? If she were involved she wouldn't care so much. At least that's what I think."

"But I agree Mrs. Oliver isn't very friendly," Violet said. "What I don't get is why she's so ready to cancel the magic show. It's a long tradition of the Greenfield Magic Shop to host the show. Those newspaper clippings on her wall go back years and years."

The Disappearing Trail

"Let's face it," Henry said, "we don't know much about the Amazing Arthur's new magic trick. We're only guessing. But he's missing. We found the big mirror smashed into pieces, and we're pretty sure someone cut themselves on the broken glass. That's what we know for sure."

Violet shrugged. "I guess we need to keep investigating."

As they left the table, Benny went over to the water fountain where Watch was patiently waiting. "You're such a good boy, Watch. It's all right if you're not a bloodhound."

Henry paid for lunch, and then the children walked through the summer crowds back to the magic shop.

CHAPTER 8

A Confession

The Greenfield Magic Shop was still hectic with kids roaming the aisles. Their voices were loud and full of wild laughter. No parents were in sight. No one was at the register.

"I wonder where Mrs. Oliver is," said Violet. "I don't see her anywhere, do you?"

"I hope *she* hasn't disappeared now!" Jessie said.

"Maybe she's at lunch," Benny grinned. "She might've been hungry like we were."

Henry laughed. "That sure was a good lunch, wasn't it Benny?"

Since Henry was taller than his siblings, he could see over the rows of toys and props. He noticed an adult on the far side of the store. He could just see a gray head of curly hair.

"I think Mrs. Oliver is over there," Henry said. He led them to a corner where a display of plastic spiders and lizards had spilled into the aisle. Magnetic coins and rings had fallen into a pile.

Mrs. Oliver was organizing a box of insects. A carton of trick thumbs and fingers had also been knocked over. One by one she was returning each prop to its proper box. She did not seem to be in a hurry. She looked up at the children but did not smile. Her eyes were red, as if she had been crying.

"Can we help you clean this up?" Violet asked. "This looks like a lot of work."

"We're happy to help," said Jessie.

"That would be lovely, children. Thank you," said Mrs. Oliver.

While the Aldens searched the floor for other tiny creatures, Henry asked if the Amazing Arthur had shown up.

"Not yet," Mrs. Oliver replied. "I've been here all day. If he were here, he'd be managing those wild kids or helping me organize things."

"Are you still thinking of canceling the magic

show, Mrs. Oliver?" Violet wanted to know. "It's just a few days away."

"Still thinking about it," the woman answered. "At the very least I'm considering letting Captain Cannon run it. He's so insistent. It's almost like he caused the disappearance of the Amazing Arthur just so he can be in charge."

Mrs. Oliver sighed deeply then put her head in her hands. "Honestly I don't know what to do."

Jessie patted Mrs. Oliver's shoulder. "Is it possible you could run the magic show?"

"Don't you know most of the tricks?" Benny asked.

"Of course I do," Mrs. Oliver said. "I grew up in a family that performed many, many magic tricks. All the time. At the breakfast nook before I went to school. At dinner while we had dessert. During Thanksgiving when all our relatives sat around the table. I wore a darling little cape with sparkles. My magic wand glowed in the dark."

"That sounds like fun," said Jessie.

"It was, actually. As long as it was only in front of my friends and my family. I was terrified of getting up on the stage with everyone looking at me."

A Confession

Henry burst out, "I feel the same way!"

"I understand completely," said Mrs. Oliver. "For me, growing up was about magic all the time. So I know the secret tricks."

"All of them?" Henry asked.

"Well, I need to back up a bit there," she said. "I only know the tricks my family performed. I don't know other magicians' tricks. The Amazing Arthur didn't tell me about his brand new trick. I knew he would magically appear, but I never asked for the details. So I guess to answer your question, Henry, I don't know all the tricks after all."

Violet said, "Maybe you can run the magic show anyway? If you held it here, it could be a smaller affair. Henry's been practicing so he'll be ready to perform. He won't let us see what he's really doing."

"Magician's code," Benny said with pride for his brother. "You can trust him, Mrs. Oliver. He doesn't give anything away."

The bell over the entry door rang. Mrs. Oliver and the Aldens looked up to see who might be coming in.

"More kids," she said. "I cannot believe parents

just drop them off and think I'll babysit. Listen, nice talking to you four. I need to get up to the counter."

Henry volunteered to finish cleaning up the spilled props.

"I accept. Thank you, Henry. You children certainly are decent. Please stop by the register before you leave, okay? I have some very fine peppermints I like to share with polite children."

While Benny picked up the rubber tarantulas, his sisters gathered the plastic mice and frogs. Henry stabilized the display rack. "Here we go. Hopefully it won't fall over if anyone runs by it now."

Jessie spoke in a soft voice. She looked toward the counter where Mrs. Oliver was helping an elderly couple. "You know, I don't think Mrs. Oliver's involved," she said. "She actually seems nice but just stressed out."

Henry said, "I think you're right, Jessie."

The bell over the door jingled again.

Violet whispered, "You won't believe who just walked in."

A man in a pirate costume hobbled up to the counter where Mrs. Oliver stood.

A Confession

"It's Captain Cannon!" Benny said in a loud whisper. "And he's limping!"

"Yeah, he sure is," said Violet.

"Let's go talk to him," said Jessie.

The Aldens finished tidying a display of trick soda cans. Then they went up to Captain Cannon.

Violet was rather timid, but she said, "Excuse me, Captain Cannon?"

"What is it?" he asked.

Violet pointed to the bloody rag wrapped around his hand. "Did you hurt yourself?" she asked. "Are you all right?"

"Fine. I'm just fine!" he grumbled. "It's an addition to my costume. What do you kids care, anyway?"

The Alden children looked at one another. Jessie was the first to say what they were thinking.

"Captain Cannon, were you in the community center this morning?" Jessie asked.

The magician in the pirate costume gave the children an angry pirate stare. "What's it to you?" he said.

"Well, we, uh," Violet hesitated.

Then Jessie said, "We were there. We found

boxes knocked over. We heard a loud crash, and then we found the big mirror smashed to smithereens. It's the one that was here the other day, by the front of the store."

"What! It's broken?" said Mrs. Oliver. "What on Earth happened?"

"That's what we're trying to find out," Henry said.

Captain Cannon stomped his pirate boot. He huffed and blew out his cheeks. "Oh, all right. If you must know, yes, I was there this morning. I was looking through the props. Since I haven't been able to find the Amazing Arthur, I thought I might be able to figure out his big new trick."

He took another deep breath. "I really want the magic show to go on."

"We do too," said Henry. "I've been practicing my act."

"Then you understand," said Captain Cannon. "That's why I like to stay in my costume. To keep in the mood. So anyway, this morning I went to the community center before it opened. The side door was unlocked. I thought I was alone until I heard you kids. I hope you realize how loud you are, by the way."

"We need to practice whispering," Benny said in a quiet voice to Violet.

"I was so startled to hear you kids wander into the auditorium and get on the stage that I got flustered. I didn't want you to see me. When I tried to hurry away, I crashed into the boxes. It was bad enough that I knocked them over and banged my knee. Man that hurt! Then I bumped into that big mirror. I watched it fall. It felt like slow motion. I tried to catch the mirror, but it broke. That's how I cut my hand."

Mrs. Oliver crossed her arms. She looked angry. "I'll have you know it was a very expensive mirror, Captain Cannon. My grandfather left it to me."

"It was an accident. I'm very sorry, Mrs. Oliver. I'll work to repay you." Captain Cannon looked at his bandaged hand. "Do you have another mirror I can purchase? One I can take to the community center, to replace the one I broke?"

"I'm afraid I don't," Mrs. Oliver answered.

"Oh, never mind!" said the pirate magician as he limped out of the shop.

Mrs. Oliver said, "Well, that was interesting."

A Confession

Jessie said, "Mrs. Oliver, do you know any tricks the big mirror could be used for?"

"Why do you ask?" the woman said.

Jessie checked her little notebook of clues. "I wonder if we can figure out the trick. Maybe then we can find a way for the Amazing Arthur to reappear. I bet that's why Captain Cannon is looking for another mirror."

"You might be right," said Henry. "He really seems to want the show to go on."

Henry's Theory

After Captain Cannon stomped out of the magic shop, Mrs. Oliver groaned. "Sorry to say this, but he makes me nervous. I'm glad you went to the community center. If you hadn't heard him crashing around, I might never have known what happened to my grandfather's mirror."

"He did come to see if he could replace the mirror," Jessie said. "He seemed genuine about it being an accident."

"I hope he pays you back, Mrs. Oliver," said Benny.

"Even if he does," she said, "he'll never be able to replace that mirror. It was a family heirloom, priceless. I grew up watching my grandparents create illusions with it."

Henry's Theory

"Did you ever see them appear and disappear?" Henry asked the store owner.

"Oh my goodness, yes!" Mrs. Oliver replied. "Many, many times. It became their most famous trick. People in the audience would clap and yell with surprise. I was proud to watch."

Henry turned his attention to the front of the shop, where the mirror had stood. He asked, "Did your grandparents show you how they did it?"

"Never," said Mrs. Oliver. "They stopped performing by the time I thought to ask. Oh... gosh...you know what? I did see my father perform that trick once at the house. But he used a hidden door we had. Most buildings don't come with those these days."

"So what do we do now?" Benny asked. "How can we find the Amazing Arthur?"

Jessie opened her little notebook. She flipped through the pages and read the clues they had found. With her pen she checked off each one. "So here we are," she said. "We know Captain Cannon knocked over the boxes at the community center. And we know he broke the mirror."

"And we know he left the trail of dripping blood," Benny said.

"I used to think Captain Cannon was guilty of causing the Amazing Arthur to disappear," said Violet. "But now I think Captain Cannon is just jealous. He's definitely trying to be the best magician in Greenfield."

"Then where did the Amazing Arthur go?" Jessie asked. "The newspaper reporters haven't come up with any tragic stories. No crime that anyone knows of."

Henry shrugged. "That's the big question," he said. "Since everything with magic is an illusion, maybe we can solve this. We just need to figure out which illusion the Amazing Arthur was trying to master."

"One minute he wasn't anywhere in the shop. The next minute," Benny snapped his fingers, "there he was."

Henry walked up to the front of the store where the mirror had been. "Jessie, do you remember exactly where the mirror was? Was it here?" He tapped the floor with his foot.

"Yes," she answered. "I think it was right there. But how does that help our investigation?" She held her pen, ready to jot down more details.

"It's sort of like working backward," Henry explained. "If we can figure out *how* the illusion is done, maybe we can find the Amazing Arthur."

Henry looked carefully at the wall, up and down. Now he snapped his fingers too. "Mrs. Oliver, would you happen to have another big mirror somewhere? Since the one at the community center is broken? You told Captain Cannon you don't sell them."

"That's true," she said. Then her face registered surprise, as if she just remembered something. "You know what? It's almost closing time. After everyone's gone I want to show you something."

***

Mrs. Oliver went to the front of the shop. A sign dangled in the window. She turned it so that anyone walking along the sidewalk could read it: "Closed. Please come back tomorrow." Then she said, "Come with me, kids. I have something that might interest you." She motioned for them to follow her.

She led them into the storeroom. It was smaller than the magic shop itself, but it was packed floor to ceiling with shelves and boxes. She went over to a large crate the size of a refrigerator. "Can you help me move this please?" she asked.

Henry and Jessie helped Mrs. Oliver ease the crate away from the wall. Propped behind it was what looked like a large painting. It was covered in paper made from brown grocery sacks.

"How will a painting help a magic trick?" Violet asked.

"It's not a painting, Violet. Look." Mrs. Oliver carefully peeled away the protective paper.

"A mirror!" cried Jessie. "It's so pretty."

"Yes." Mrs. Oliver was smiling now. She stepped back to admire it. "It's from my grandmother's dressing room."

"Wow," said Benny. "It's the fanciest mirror I've ever seen."

An elegant mirror stood before them. It was as tall as Mrs. Oliver and two feet wide. Roses and daisies had been engraved into the wood frame. The flowers had been painted in swirls of pink, white,

and purple. Vines in shades of green swirled along the sides, up to the top and down to the bottom.

"It's beautiful, Mrs. Oliver," Jessie said.

"Indeed, it is," the woman said. "I had completely forgotten about this. I put it out of my mind when the old family house was sold. So many treasured antiques and thick rugs were packed up and put here for storage. I was quite sad to see the empty rooms and bare floors."

Henry glanced around the storeroom. "It looks like you put a lot of those things in here. I can see the boxes of props and costumes. And over there is a rolltop desk. And fancy chairs."

"You're right, Henry," Mrs. Oliver said. "And under that tarp over there is a maple dining table from Revolutionary War days. As children my brothers, sisters, cousins, and I made forts under that table. We played hide-and-seek in that grand old house and practiced tricks. We loved trying out practical jokes on one another."

"That sounds like a lot of fun," said Violet.

"Oh, it was. I had a charmed childhood," said Mrs. Oliver. "Anyway I remember my grandmother—I called her Nana—insisting I take care of this mirror. In addition to being a magician, she was an artist. She was extremely creative. As you can see she painted this frame with red and white roses and with lots of purple. It was her favorite color."

Mrs. Oliver glanced at Violet with affection. "I can see you favor the color too," she said, gesturing at Violet's purple hair ribbons and T-shirt.

"I do!" Violet cried. "I really like purple. My sleeping bag is lavender, and so is my bathing suit."

"Even her toothbrush is purple!" Benny exclaimed.

Mrs. Oliver smiled. "This mirror brings back happy memories," she said. Then she turned to the children. "Now where were we?"

"May we borrow this for our experiment?" Henry asked Mrs. Oliver.

"It's not as big as the other one," Jessie observed. "The mirror that broke."

"True," said Mrs. Oliver. "My Nana was smaller than my grandfather. Rather petite, you might say. She gazed at herself every morning before she got dressed. I remember helping her fasten her cape on many occasions before magic shows.

People often said that Nana and I looked alike. She had gray curly hair like I do now."

Mrs. Oliver looked at the children. "Oh, listen to me carry on. I'm sorry! Henry," she said, "do you think you can experiment with my grandmother's mirror without breaking it? I can't bear another catastrophe."

"Yes. We'll be super careful, Mrs. Oliver," he assured her. "And since the shop is closed, no little kids can run into us."

"All right then," she said. "Can you four get it from here without dropping it?"

"We're good at stuff like this," Benny said. He and his siblings regarded one another with hopeful grins. Then Henry, Jessie, Violet, and Benny each carefully took one side of the mirror. They lifted it, hanging on tight, and shuffled it out of the storeroom.

A New Surprise

With the magic shop closed, it was quiet. No restless children ran around the aisles. There were no customers.

The Aldens carried Mrs. Oliver's beautiful mirror from the storeroom. It was heavy. They set it down to rest a moment, then continued up to the front of the store. There they gently settled the mirror into its upright position as Mrs. Oliver watched.

"Right here," said Jessie. "I'm sure this is where the other mirror stood." She and Henry took hold of the top of the mirror until it rested safely on its stand.

They stood thoughtfully.

Henry looked down the main aisle toward the stage. Then he looked up at Mrs. Oliver's mirror.

The distance was short, about the length of a school bus.

"This is interesting," he said. "Somehow it *looked* like the Amazing Arthur came out of the front mirror the other day. Hey, Jessie, I have an idea."

Jessie followed Henry to the back of the shop. The stage butted up against a wall of pine paneling. When Henry ran his fingers over the wood, she did the same. Together they inspected the wall.

"Hmm," said Jessie. "I think I know what's here."

"What? What?" cried Benny. "I want to help too." He hurried to them and copied what they were doing. He touched the wall down by his feet then as high as he could go on his toes. "Hmm," he said, mimicking Jessie.

Now Violet hurried down the aisle to the stage. She touched the wall too. "What are you looking for, Henry?" she asked.

As Henry ran his fingers over a narrow section of the wall, he leaned closer. He squinted. "Look at this!" he said. He drew his thumb over a narrow up-and-down crack. He quickly pressed it, and the tiny crack revealed itself to be the edge of a door.

A New Surprise

With a quiet *whoosh* the door slowly—very slowly— slid open.

"A pocket door!" he cried. "And a hidden room."

Mrs. Oliver said, "My goodness. I had no idea this was here."

"Why is it called a pocket door?" Violet asked.

"Because the wall is like a pocket," Mrs. Oliver answered. "It keeps the door hidden. The one my grandparents had in their house was beautiful carved wood. It separated their parlor from their den."

"How did you know this was here, Henry?" Jessie asked.

"It was something Mrs. Oliver said," Henry replied. "She mentioned hidden doors aren't common these days."

Violet gasped. "But since the magic shop has been around so long, you thought it might have one?"

Henry nodded.

Benny peeked into the hidden room. "Guys, look!" he cried. "Is this another mirror?" He waved his hand in front of a full-length piece of glass. The glass reflected his hand, then it reflected the curious faces of his siblings. It was indeed a mirror.

Now the children turned to look up the aisle. Mrs. Oliver's mirror at the front of the store showed the four children waving. They smiled at their reflections. It appeared like they were magically standing inside of the mirror.

Henry breathed a sigh of relief. "That's it! It's an optical illusion," he said. "I thought so."

Now Violet stepped into the dark space behind the mirror. "I wonder what's in here," she said. Henry followed her, then Violet and Benny. Just as Mrs. Oliver joined them, there was another soft *whoosh*. The secret door was closing behind them! They were now shut inside a dark passageway.

"What just happened?" Jessie whispered. "It's pitch black."

"Where are we?" said Violet.

"I wish I had my flashlight," Benny said. He grabbed Violet's hand for comfort.

"Let's keep going," said Henry. "I'm sure we'll be okay."

The Aldens and Mrs. Oliver continued single file. In the darkness they stepped cautiously. Just as they rounded a corner, they saw a crack of light on the floor in front of them. Another door! When Henry pushed it open, light flooded the passageway.

They gasped with surprise. Before them was a small room. The Amazing Arthur was sitting on a stool. He wore jeans, a sweatshirt, and a baseball cap. He did not look like a magician.

For one long moment everyone was quiet.

The Amazing Arthur looked down at his tennis shoes with embarrassment. "This is awkward," he said. "I'm so sorry for worrying you, Mrs. Oliver. I'm sorry I missed your lessons, Henry."

"Have you been here the whole time?" Henry asked.

Jessie looked at her notebook. "It's been two days," she said. "We've been wondering about you all this time."

"Why did you hide?" asked Benny.

The Amazing Arthur replied, "I've been trying to figure out how to do my appearing act at the community center. There's no hidden door there. I just couldn't figure it out. I was frustrated, and I didn't want to disappoint anyone. I'm sorry," he repeated.

A New Surprise

"Why didn't you just tell me?" Mrs. Oliver asked the magician.

The Amazing Arthur sighed. His shoulders slumped. "I didn't want to break the magician's code," he replied. "You were so set against having the magic show here. I was just trying to think of another way to do the trick. I didn't want to give away the secret."

Violet pointed to a pile of blue papers on top of a small table in the corner. "The flyers," she said. "They're right here."

Benny said, "So no one stole them?"

"Well, I confess I took the flyers," said the Amazing Arthur.

"Why?" Violet asked.

"I was worried," the Amazing Arthur continued. "I worried the whole town would show up at the community center for the magic show."

"I thought that's what you wanted," Mrs. Oliver said.

"Yes and no," he answered. "Picture this. Parents and kids buy their tickets. They first stop at the popcorn stand and then buy sodas. Excited, they file into the auditorium to their seats. They wait for the lights to dim. They wait for that huge red curtain to part."

"I like this part," said Benny.

The Amazing Arthur suddenly looked sad. "But if I had then appeared on the stage, under the spotlight, well—"

"I think I understand," said Henry. "Everyone would be looking at you. They'd be expecting you to do a fantastic trick. The one here." Henry picked up one of the flyers and read the announcement as he had the other day. "'Come one, come all. The Amazing Arthur will surprise you by appearing out of thin air!'"

Now Mrs. Oliver was nodding. "The community center isn't like this magic shop," she admitted. "If I'd known about this secret room, I would have understood. Now I know why you were so upset."

"I'd rather the show be canceled," said the Amazing Arthur. "That's why I took the flyers. I'm so embarrassed. I'm sorry, really sorry, Mrs. Oliver. I was so hopeful that I'd figure out another way to perform the trick."

A New Surprise

"You stayed here overnight?" Mrs. Oliver asked.

"Yes. I hid in here and waited until you had locked up. Until it was dark. Then I used a flashlight so no one out on the sidewalks would see me inside the shop. I practiced and practiced. I tried to imagine myself on that big stage in the community center with no secret door."

"But how did you go back and forth without one of my new keys?" Mrs. Oliver asked.

Benny jumped up. "Because he never left the shop! Is that right, sir?"

"You are correct," the Amazing Arthur answered. He pointed to a cozy corner with a cot and sleeping bag. A small night table made from a box held a reading lamp. A pair of sparkly shoes were tucked under a bench.

Mrs. Oliver said, "So that's why I didn't see you leave. I locked the doors. I was the only one with a key. I assumed you were wandering around town or something. Hmm." She thought a moment. "Did you take the mirror over to the community center?"

"I did," said the Amazing Arthur. "During the day when you were busy in the storeroom, I carried the mirror out the side door. My pickup was parked in the alley, so I delivered the mirror and quickly returned."

The group was quiet for several moments.

Finally Benny asked about one of his favorite topics. "Didn't you get hungry all this time?"

The Amazing Arthur patted his stomach and laughed. "I brought peanut butter sandwiches and apples," he said.

Mrs. Oliver sighed. Then she laughed too. "I'm sorry I said so many grumpy things about you."

The Amazing Arthur smiled a tired smile. "It's okay, Mrs. Oliver. I don't blame you for being grumpy. I should have told you. But I just don't see how I can do this at the community center."

The group was quiet again. Then Jessie remembered something. She said, "Mrs. Oliver, the other day you told us you think change is good."

"Yes. I still do."

"And that you have reasons," Jessie went on, "for having the magic show at the community center."

Mrs. Oliver moved to sit on the bench. She rubbed the small of her back like she was tired and sore. "Yes, I have several reasons," she answered. "As I said before, I'm trying to run a business. All these jokes and tricks make it a fun place, not a serious place. But—"

The Aldens listened.

"But at this moment," Mrs. Oliver went on, "I'm reminded how much I like fun. I love magic. I love seeing an excited audience. I love hearing the laughter of children."

"Oh, so do I!" said the Amazing Arthur. His eyebrows lifted as he regarded the Aldens. "I believe we all do," he said.

"Yes!" Benny answered for his brother and sisters.

"Are you changing your mind, Mrs. Oliver?" Violet asked. "Will you let the magic show be here?"

"I've been too focused on the business side," the store owner replied. "But I also realize something else that bothers me. Now that I think about it, that is."

"Mrs. Oliver, what is it?" Henry asked gently.

In a soft voice she said, "I feel guilty admitting this."

The Mystery in the Magic Shop

The Amazing Arthur leaned forward to hear. Henry, Jessie, Violet, and Benny did the same.

Finally Mrs. Oliver continued. "The main reason I want to move the magic show to the community center is because they have janitors. And I could use the help with cleaning."

The Amazing Arthur laughed. "Makes sense to me."

Benny said, "We saw a janitor there and reported the broken mirror. I bet he swept it up."

"And sweeps the big stage too," said Henry.

"You see," said Mrs. Oliver, "putting on a magic show is a lot of work. Too much work. Setting everything up and moving displays. Dusting. Cleaning before the show and cleaning after everyone goes home. Someone always manages to clomp around in dirty boots."

Violet said, "I understand that. Our housekeeper, Mrs. McGregor, gets frustrated when we track muddy shoes into her clean kitchen."

"Then you do understand," said Mrs. Oliver.

The Alden children listened.

"I used to love magic shows," Mrs. Oliver

explained. "All during my childhood my parents were so happy performing together. I did some tricks with them. But mostly I had to sweep up confetti afterward and scrape chewing gum off the floor. Can you believe that? Spitting out gum onto beautiful old wooden floors? Honestly."

With another weary sigh Mrs. Oliver said, "Do you realize how hard it is to capture balloons that have floated into the rafters? Especially after they pop and the pieces of rubber stick to the wood? It's a terrible mess. I'm not getting any younger, you know. Climbing on a ladder these days scares me." She patted her gray curls.

After a moment Henry said, "What if you have a great crew to help set up?"

"And clean afterward?" Jessie said.

"I'm good at sweeping," Benny boasted. "I get lots of practice at home."

"I'm sure you do, Benny," said Mrs. Oliver.

The children glanced at one another with concern. They waited.

After a long moment Mrs. Oliver smiled. "All right," she said. "I accept your help. We can have the show here. But I have one very serious question."

"So do I," said the Amazing Arthur.

"Are we good at keeping secrets?" Violet guessed. "Will we honor the magician's code?"

"You read my mind, my dear," said Mrs. Oliver.

"Mine too," said the Amazing Arthur.

Henry answered first. "Absolutely, we'll honor the magician's code," he said.

Violet agreed. "Definitely," she said.

"Yes, sir!" Benny cried. "We're good at keeping secrets."

Jessie held up her notebook. "I won't even write it down," she said. "That way no one will be able to read it."

"I trust you children," said the Amazing Arthur.

"So do I," Mrs. Oliver said. "All right then. I need to redo the flyers to announce that the Greenfield Magic Show will be held here. The Amazing Arthur will perform his new fabulous trick. And our newest magician, Henry Alden, will also perform. Will you be ready this weekend, Henry?"

Henry beamed. "You bet," he said. "I can't wait!"

Read on for a sneak preview of

The Big Spill Rescue

**the first book of
The Boxcar Children®
Endangered Animals,
an all-new series!**

"I want to touch a shark!" called six-year-old Benny Alden.

"Shh!" Benny's sister Jessie put a finger to her lips. "The sign says we should whisper."

Benny put his hand to his mouth. Then he whispered, "I want to touch a shark!" just as excitedly, but quieter.

The Aldens were at the Port Elizabeth Aquarium. In front of them, a shallow tank stretched across the room. Inside, small sharks and stingrays swam lazily among rocks and plants. A sign above read "Touch Tank." That meant visitors were welcome to reach into the tank through the open top.

Grandfather put his hand on Benny's shoulder. "You'll get a chance, but first we have to learn the rules."

"That's right," said Isaiah Young. "Listen to Kayla, she'll explain."

Mr. Young was an old friend of Grandfather's. The Aldens were staying with him while they visited Port Elizabeth. Kayla, his daughter, was their unofficial guide to the aquarium.

"Thanks, Dad." Kayla spoke softly. "We whisper so we won't frighten the animals. You should also move slowly. Put your hand right under the surface of the water. Hold it there with your palm down."

Kayla wore a blue collared shirt, and her tiny braids were pulled back into a ponytail. She was a biologist and knew all about the animals they were going to see at the aquarium. It was clear she knew what she was talking about, and some other visitors even gathered around to listen.

The four children followed Kayla's lead. A stingray swam toward them. As it rose in the water, Violet's hand stroked across its back. She tried to keep quiet but let out a tiny squeal of joy and excitement. "It's smooth and slippery," she said.

"It didn't touch me," Benny said sadly.

"Be patient," Grandfather said.

"Are there other rules?" Jessie asked. She was twelve and liked to make notes about everything she learned. She couldn't write in her notebook with her hand in the water, but she'd try to remember what she learned for later.

"Don't try to grab the animals," Kayla said. "And don't try to touch their bellies or tails. Instead, touch their backs."

"What happens if you touch a shark's tail?" Benny asked. "Will it bite?"

Kayla smiled. "These sharks won't bite. There are about four hundred species of sharks in the world, and most are small and gentle, like these. You can handle them easily."

"We still need to treat them with respect," Henry said. At fourteen, he was the oldest of the Alden children.

"That's right," Kayla said. "We should treat all animals with respect. Here at the touch tank, the sharks and rays will hide if you scare them. But if you are calm and gentle, they'll get curious and come out."

"I don't want to scare them," Benny said. "I want to make friends."

Benny held his hand under the water. His body wanted to squirm, but he tried to stay very still. A speckled shark as long as his arm swam toward him. Benny held his breath. The shark nosed at his hand, and Benny got nervous. Then it slid past, letting Benny pet down its back.

"I touched one!" Benny grinned and clapped his hands together. Water from his wet hand sprayed into his face. He wiped himself off with his shirt sleeve as the other children laughed quietly.

After a few more minutes at the touch tank, Kayla asked, "Shall we move on?"

Everyone agreed. They were excited to see the other animals at the aquarium. After the children had washed and dried their hands, Kayla led the way to the next room.

Violet walked beside her. "We don't get to touch wild animals very often," she said. "I've been to a petting barn at the zoo, but those animals aren't wild." Ten-year-old Violet loved animals. She hoped she'd get a chance to draw some during their visit to Port Elizabeth.

"You shouldn't touch animals in the wild," Kayla said. "It can be dangerous. They could hurt you, or you could hurt them. The aquarium chooses animals that are safe for the touch tank, and the tank gives them places to hide if they feel shy. The workers also keep the tank clean and watch for any sign of disease."

"That sounds like a lot of work," Violet said. "Why not let people look but not touch?"

"Good question," said Kayla. "Many people are afraid of sharks and rays, but here they see these animals aren't so dangerous. Maybe after this, your little brother will fall in love with sharks. Maybe he'll become a shark researcher someday."

"I could do that!" Benny said. "I already made friends with that speckled one."

They made their way into a glass tunnel. On the other side of the glass, water filled a huge tank. It felt like they were underwater with the fish! This tank held larger animals. Some of the fish were as long as a person was tall. At the bottom, crabs scuttled between sea urchins and coral.

Violet pointed through the glass. "Oh, that one is pretty. It looks like an orca, but it's too small. Is it a baby?"

"That is a Hector's dolphin," Kayla said.

The dolphin was mostly black. It had white from its chin down its belly. The black-and-white pattern had reminded Violet of an orca, which she knew was the largest member of the dolphin family.

"Hector's dolphins are the smallest marine dolphins in the world," Kayla said. "They are very rare and very endangered."

Benny frowned. "Are they in-dangered from people?"

"The word is *endangered*," Jessie said.

"Endangered means a species is at very great risk," Kayla said. "Only about seven thousand Hector's dolphins still live in the wild. If we don't help them, they might all die out. Then they would be all gone—extinct."

"That's awful," Benny said.

"Don't worry, Benny," said Henry. "Lots of people help protect animals like this. Right, Kayla?"

"That's right!" Kayla said. "There are many

conservation groups that help. I work with one called Protectors of Animals Worldwide, or PAW."

Violet watched the dolphin as it swooped through the water. It swam close to the glass. Then it turned on its side, flicked its tail, and zipped away. It circled back around and wiggled as it passed by once more.

"It's dancing!" Benny said. He went up to the glass and started wiggling, trying to copy the dolphin's moves.

"You called this a marine dolphin," Violet said. "Marine means it lives in the ocean, right?"

"That's right," Kayla said. "Most dolphins live in the ocean, but a few live in rivers."

Benny spun around. "Will we see one of these dolphins in the ocean?"

"I don't think so." Kayla smiled. "Hector's dolphins live near New Zealand."

"That's on the other side of the world," Henry explained.

Benny sighed. "That's a long way. Maybe someday we can go."

"That would be quite an adventure,"

Grandfather said.

"I like adventures!" Benny raised his arms over his head as a sea turtle swam up to the glass. It looked like it wondered what Benny was doing. "We've had a lot of adventures," Benny told Kayla.

"Oh really?" she asked.

"It's true," Henry said. "We like to help people and solve mysteries."

"We like to help animals too," Violet added.

"I try to help animals," Kayla said. "I don't think I've ever solved a mystery though."

Benny smiled up at her. "That's okay. Maybe we'll find one for you while we're here."

Kayla laughed.

Grandfather said, "Don't be surprised if it happens. My grandkids always find something to get into."

The Aldens' adventures had started when the children ran away from home. After their parents had died, they'd heard their grandfather was mean, so they hid in the woods and lived in an old boxcar they found. That had been their first adventure. Then they met their grandfather and found out he was very kind. He brought the children to live with him in Greenfield, Connecticut. The children still liked to hang out in the boxcar—and they still had plenty of adventures.

Benny skipped through the room. "Maybe someday I'll get to travel all over the world. I'll see animals and help them."

"Those are very good goals," Kayla said.

Jessie pulled out her notebook. "Can you tell me more about conservation? It means trying to protect nature, right?"

Kayla nodded. "PAW has programs around the world. We try to save animal species, and that means we have to protect the land. After all, you can't protect animals if they don't have a safe and healthy place to live. Everything in nature is connected."

"What do you mean?" Benny asked.

"Say a factory dumps chemicals onto the ground," Kayla said. "The chemicals can wash into a river. They can flow into lakes or all the way to the ocean. What happens if you drop a plastic bag outside? It might blow miles and miles to the coast. It could get into the water and choke a sea turtle or seal."

"That's terrible," Violet said.

"We're always careful to throw away our garbage," Henry said.

"That's important," Kayla said. "Environmental groups like mine try to educate people on things like that. We work with local communities. We work with governments. Like I said, everything is connected. People are part of that web."

Violet looked back at the dolphin and drew in her sketchbook. It was hard to draw something that moved so quickly. "I hope more people come and see animals like the Hector's dolphin," she said.

"Many people love dolphins," Kayla answered. "Most people don't know about all the different dolphin species. They don't realize some are so rare they might disappear forever. Aquariums help teach people about all the animals in danger."

"It's sad that there are so many of them that need help," Violet said, putting down her pencil.

Kayla put her hand on the girl's shoulder. "It is sad. But isn't it nice that people want to help?

Come on to the next room. We'll meet another species. This one is really *cool*."

Benny dashed ahead. "Penguins!"

In the next room, penguins played in a large area behind glass. They waddled across rocks and dove into a pool of water. Through the glass, visitors could see them swimming underwater. Violet plopped down cross-legged. She held her sketchbook in her lap and drew.

"We have African penguins and rockhoppers," Kayla said. "These are the African penguins. Rockhoppers have funny yellow feathers on their heads."

"They're adorable," Jessie said. "Are they endangered?"

"Sadly, yes," Kayla said. "Of the eighteen species of penguin, ten are endangered. Others are vulnerable. That means they aren't endangered yet, but there aren't as many as we'd like. Rockhopper penguins are vulnerable. African penguins are endangered."

The group spent some time watching the penguins, then Kayla led them outside, where a railing surrounded a huge pool. Inside were the biggest animals yet. "These are beluga whales," Kayla said. "They are found around Alaska and other northern areas."

The Aldens watched the three pale gray whales swim. One came close to peer at them. It had a bulging, rounded forehead. Its mouth seemed to be smiling.

"I thought whales were really, really big," Benny said.

"These are one of the smaller whale species," Kayla said.

Jessie read the sign. "They're still eleven to fifteen feet long. That's twice as long as Grandfather is tall, and the adults weigh more than one thousand pounds!" She made notes.

"I bet they have to eat a lot." Benny rubbed his stomach. "Like me."

"They are so cute!" said Violet.

Kayla leaned her elbows on the railing. "They sure are," she said. "I love coming to the aquarium to see the whales. But we can't forget about the animals that aren't as popular or as cute. All species are important."

"Right." Jessie looked up from her notebook. She thought she understood what Kayla was saying now. "Like you said, we are all connected. Bees pollinate many foods we eat. Snakes eat mice that would eat farmers' grain. Some people don't like bees or snakes, but we need those animals too."

"Every animal should be protected." Henry agreed. "Not only the biggest or cutest ones. I'd like to know how to help those other animals too."

The other children nodded.

Kayla smiled. "I have just the idea. But we'll have to leave the aquarium. Are you ready for a new adventure?"

"Always!" Benny said. "But maybe lunch and then an adventure, okay?" He rubbed his stomach again. "I'm hungry!"

GERTRUDE CHANDLER WARNER discovered when she was teaching that many readers who like an exciting story could find no books that were both easy and fun to read. She decided to try to meet this need, and her first book, *The Boxcar Children*, quickly proved she had succeeded.

Miss Warner drew on her own experiences to write the mystery. As a child she spent hours watching trains go by on the tracks opposite her family home. She often dreamed about what it would be like to set up housekeeping in a caboose or freight car—the situation the Alden children find themselves in.

While the mystery element is central to each of Miss Warner's books, she never thought of them as strictly juvenile mysteries. She liked to stress the Aldens' independence and resourcefulness and their solid New England devotion to using up and making do. The Aldens go about most of their adventures with as little adult supervision as possible—something else that delights young readers.

Miss Warner lived in Putnam, Connecticut, until her death in 1979. During her lifetime, she received hundreds of letters from girls and boys telling her how much they liked her books.